To:
Emma and Julia

Love:
Miss Fern

ROCKRHYDIN

BY CHERYL ELIZABETH WADDELL
ILLUSTRATIONS BY JANICE PREY WOLFE
THEME SONG BY FERN CARVER MICHONSKI

Rockrhydin

Text copyright ©1986, 2012, 2013 by Cheryl Elizabeth Waddell

Illustrations copyright ©1994, 2012, 2013 by Janice Prey Wolfe

Theme song copyright ©1993 by Fern Carver Michonski

Published by Fern's Music/Fern Forest Enterprises

542 Hopmeadow Street, #120 Simsbury CT 06070

Printed and bound in Canada

Friesens Corporation of Altona, Manitoba

Library of Congress Catalog-in-Publication Data

Waddell, Cheryl Elizabeth.

Rockrhydin / by Cheryl Elizabeth Waddell: illustrated by Janice Prey Wolfe

Summary:

When a boy and his rocking horse are separated,

they discover Christmas wishes haven't any *nevers*.

[1. Christmas-Fiction. 2. Rocking Horse-Fiction. 3. Friendship-Fiction.]

I. Wolfe, Janice Prey, ill. []. Title.

2013945211

ISBN 978-0-578-12763-7

Second Edition

10 9 8 7 6 5 4 3 2 1

For Brett, Bart, and Elizabeth
—C. E. W.

For Taylor, and Bryan, Parker, Trisha, Adriana, Elisabeth, Nick
—J. P. W.

For Laura, Scott, and Kent
—F. C. M.

With loving thanks to Homer and Mary Waddell
Ernie and Carolyn Carver
Vlada and Mim Sajkovic
who never lost the belief that Christmas wishes haven't any *nevers*

www.fernsmusicforkids.com

To download the theme song, "Rockrhydin,"
written by Fern Carver Michonski, go to:
http://www.fernsmusicforkids.com

Once upon a time, a little boy named Jon Michael had a rocking horse he called Rockrhydin. Jon Michael spent many happy hours in his nursery with Rockrhydin. But as happens with little boys, one day Jon Michael was not so little anymore. In fact, his legs were rapidly outgrowing Rockrhydin. Everyone, including Jon Michael's aunts and uncles, exclaimed, "My, what a big boy you are!"

His parents moved him into a larger bedroom where he slept in a big mahogany bed with four tall posts. He stayed up later in the evening with the grown-ups, and read books with more words than pictures. His grandmother gave him a violin that had belonged to his great grandfather. Twice a week a man with a bushy white moustache came to teach Jon Michael how to play the fine instrument.

Jon Michael enjoyed his life as a growing boy; yet, every now and then, he would peek in his former nursery and smile at Rockrhydin.

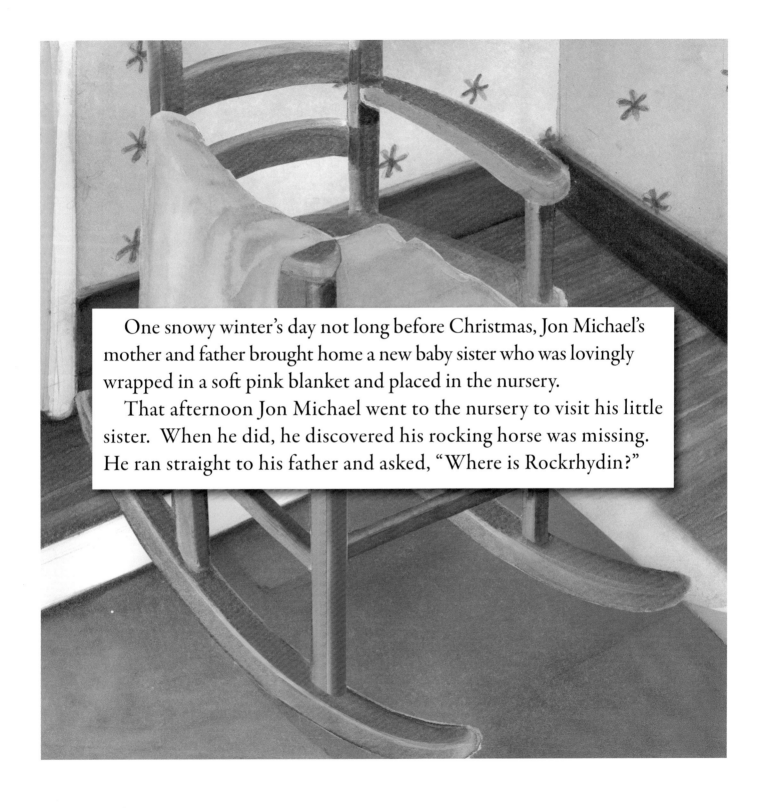

One snowy winter's day not long before Christmas, Jon Michael's mother and father brought home a new baby sister who was lovingly wrapped in a soft pink blanket and placed in the nursery.

That afternoon Jon Michael went to the nursery to visit his little sister. When he did, he discovered his rocking horse was missing. He ran straight to his father and asked, "Where is Rockrhydin?"

"He was taken away with some of your older toys the other day," answered his father. "I didn't think you'd mind. You outgrew Rockrhydin—and he was pretty worn out. His saddle was broken, his rockers were wobbly, and nothing much was left of his mane."

Jon Michael nodded his head in quiet agreement, but later went to his bedroom, shut the door, and cried.

As for Rockrhydin, he was standing in a dump at the far edge of town, his rickety rockers buried in snow. He found neither a friend nor a rider all that cold December day.

When the sun set, the crisp clear night sent shivers down Rockrhydin's spine. The stars twinkled brightly, but Rockrhydin did not see them for his eyes were downcast. Just as he was about to shut them tight forever, he heard the curious tinkling of a bell.

Rockrhydin looked up and saw a beautiful green-eyed lady standing before him. She was dressed in snow-white and wore a wreath of holly in her hair. In her hand she held a sparkling wand with a little silver bell at its tip.

"Rockrhydin," she sighed, "how sad you look this evening. I am Tanyabelle, the keeper of Christmas wishes. What wish might I grant to make your heart smile?"

"A...a...wish?" stammered the astonished rocking horse. "Any wish at all?"

"Any wish at all," she assured him.

"I wish to be with Jon Michael."

"Then it shall be done."

Tanyabelle waved her wand in a wish-granting gesture.

"No, No!" cried out Rockrhydin. "Jon Michael outgrew me and his father sent me away. If I went back, I would be sent away once again. I could wish myself real, but Jon Michael has no barn."

A tear welled up in Rockrhydin's small black eye. "I guess I will never see Jon Michael again," he sighed.

"Christmas wishes haven't any *nevers,*" said Tanyabelle, smiling kindly. "There is a way you can be with Jon Michael."

"What way?" asked Rockrhydin in an expectant tone.

"If you wouldn't mind growing smaller," she answered, "—very much smaller, I could transform you into a Christmas tree ornament. And I promise you, should I do so, I will see to it that Jon Michael, himself, hangs you on his Christmas tree."

Rockrhydin hesitated for a moment. He thought of how much bigger and bolder his world would seem. Then he thought of belonging to Jon Michael. Suddenly, he felt warm and glowing inside. For the first time in a long while, Rockrhydin smiled.

"Yes! Yes! Yes!" he sang out. "I want to be a Christmas tree ornament."

"As you wish," said Tanyabelle, gently waving her wand above Rockrhydin's head.

Rockrhydin heard the tinkling of the little silver bell.

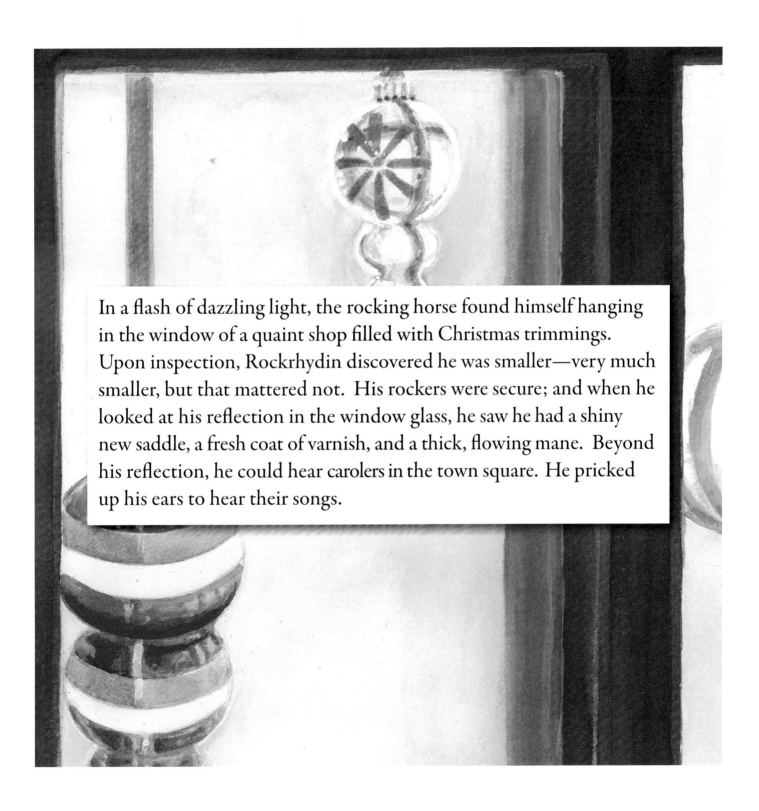

In a flash of dazzling light, the rocking horse found himself hanging in the window of a quaint shop filled with Christmas trimmings. Upon inspection, Rockrhydin discovered he was smaller—very much smaller, but that mattered not. His rockers were secure; and when he looked at his reflection in the window glass, he saw he had a shiny new saddle, a fresh coat of varnish, and a thick, flowing mane. Beyond his reflection, he could hear carolers in the town square. He pricked up his ears to hear their songs.

In a short while, large lacey snowflakes began to fall on the bustling shoppers passing by. As Rockrhydin watched them he spotted Jon Michael's father hurrying along the street. His arms were filled with brightly wrapped packages. As he drew nearer the shop, Rockrhydin's heart leapt with hope.

Jon Michael's father glanced in the window. He appeared about to go on his way when he spied the miniature rocking horse hanging there. To the delight of Rockrhydin's wondering ears, the bells on the shop's front door jingled cheerily as Jon Michael's father stepped in from the cold.

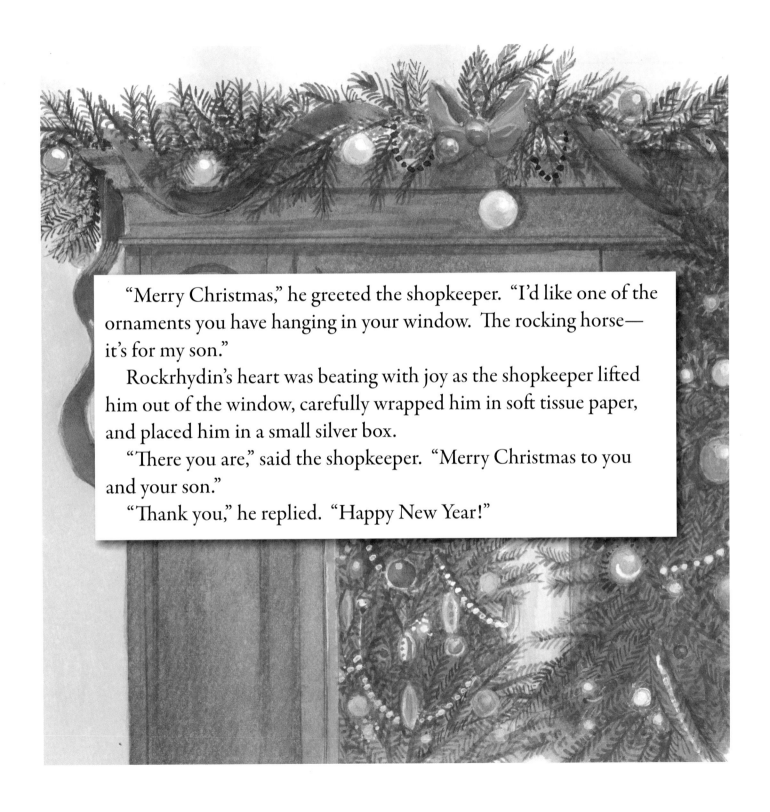

"Merry Christmas," he greeted the shopkeeper. "I'd like one of the ornaments you have hanging in your window. The rocking horse— it's for my son."

Rockrhydin's heart was beating with joy as the shopkeeper lifted him out of the window, carefully wrapped him in soft tissue paper, and placed him in a small silver box.

"There you are," said the shopkeeper. "Merry Christmas to you and your son."

"Thank you," he replied. "Happy New Year!"

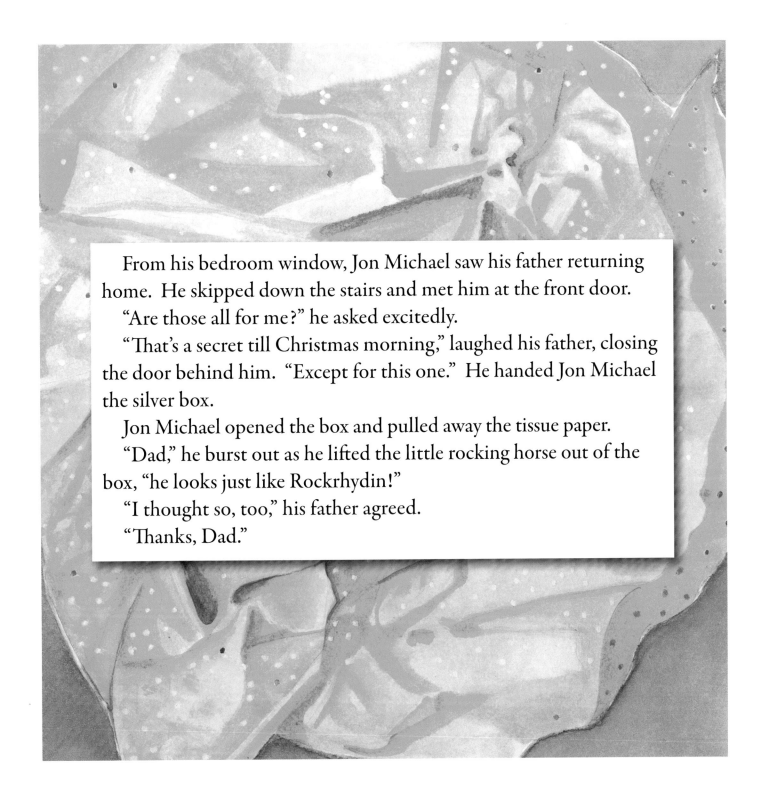

From his bedroom window, Jon Michael saw his father returning home. He skipped down the stairs and met him at the front door.

"Are those all for me?" he asked excitedly.

"That's a secret till Christmas morning," laughed his father, closing the door behind him. "Except for this one." He handed Jon Michael the silver box.

Jon Michael opened the box and pulled away the tissue paper.

"Dad," he burst out as he lifted the little rocking horse out of the box, "he looks just like Rockrhydin!"

"I thought so, too," his father agreed.

"Thanks, Dad."

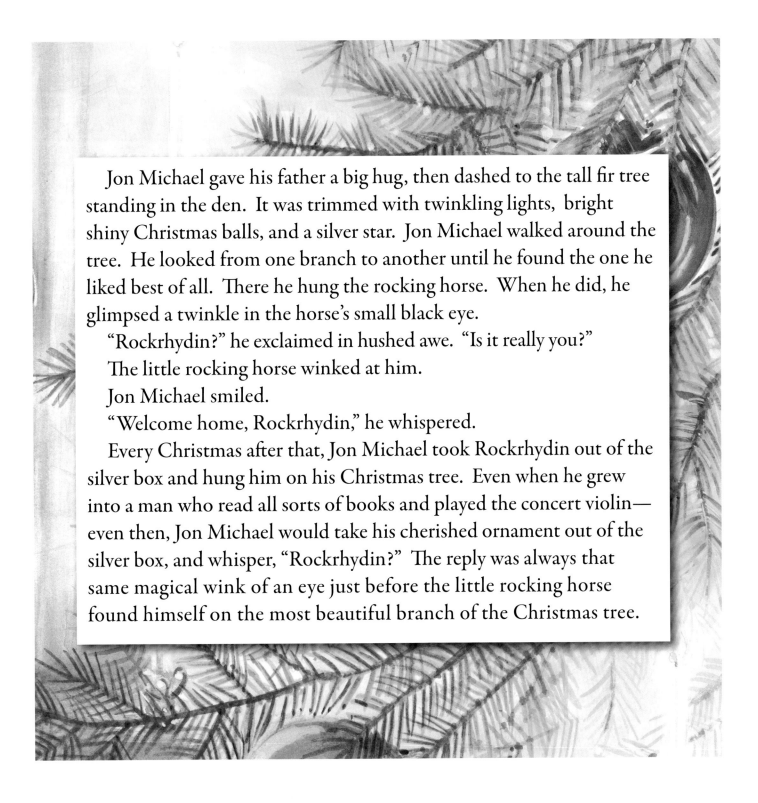

Jon Michael gave his father a big hug, then dashed to the tall fir tree standing in the den. It was trimmed with twinkling lights, bright shiny Christmas balls, and a silver star. Jon Michael walked around the tree. He looked from one branch to another until he found the one he liked best of all. There he hung the rocking horse. When he did, he glimpsed a twinkle in the horse's small black eye.

"Rockrhydin?" he exclaimed in hushed awe. "Is it really you?"

The little rocking horse winked at him.

Jon Michael smiled.

"Welcome home, Rockrhydin," he whispered.

Every Christmas after that, Jon Michael took Rockrhydin out of the silver box and hung him on his Christmas tree. Even when he grew into a man who read all sorts of books and played the concert violin— even then, Jon Michael would take his cherished ornament out of the silver box, and whisper, "Rockrhydin?" The reply was always that same magical wink of an eye just before the little rocking horse found himself on the most beautiful branch of the Christmas tree.

Epilogue

Year after merry year, miniature rocking horses have decorated the branches of Christmas trees. Some have been created by wood carvers with gentle hearts and skilled hands. Others have been made by big noisy machines. And a precious few, like Rockrhydin, have been transformed from old and broken rocking horses into treasured ornaments by the wave of Tanyabelle's wand.

The End

To download the theme song, "Rockrhydin,"
written by Fern Carver Michonski, go to:
http://www.fernsmusicforkids.com

Fern's Music™

Fern Forest Enterprises

www.fernsmusicforkids.com